Happy
HARRY'S
Café

For Emma, Elsie and Emile, and remembering my father, Harold, who told me a version of this story. Michael Rosen

JP

First published 2012 by Walker Books Ltd, 87 Vauxhall Walk, London SE11 5HJ

This edition published 2012

2 4 6 8 10 9 7 5 3 1

Text © 2012 Michael Rosen   Illustrations © 2012 Richard Holland

The right of Michael Rosen and Richard Holland to be identified as author and illustrator respectively of this work has been asserted by them in accordance with the Copyright, Designs and Patents Act 1988

This book has been typeset in Bodoni Poster Compressed

Printed in China

British Library Cataloguing in Publication Data:
a catalogue record for this book is available from the British Library

ISBN 978-1-4063-4438-7

www.walker.co.uk

WALKER BOOKS
AND SUBSIDIARIES
LONDON · BOSTON · SYDNEY · AUCKLAND

For Camilla and Evie   Richard

Michael Rosen

Happy
HARRY'S
Café

illustrated by

Richard Holland

Here's

Harry.

He works at

Happy

HARRY'S

Café.

Harry makes great

soup.

His friends run for Harry's

soup,

before Harry's

soup

runs out.

Here's
Ryan the lion.

He's in a rush. He's Rushing Ryan.

"Take it easy, Ryan," says Harry.

Here's
Jo the crow.

She's riding fast.

Jo's no Slow-Jo, oh no.

"Take it easy, Jo," says Harry.

Here's
Robin the robin.

Robin is really bobbing along.

"Take it easy, Robin," says Harry.

Here's
Matt the cat.

As fast as the wind, and faster than that.

"Take it easy, Matt," says Harry.

They're all in a hurry to have Harry's

soup.

Everyone loves Harry's

soup.

"Love the soup, Harry. Yum!"

"Mmmmm!"

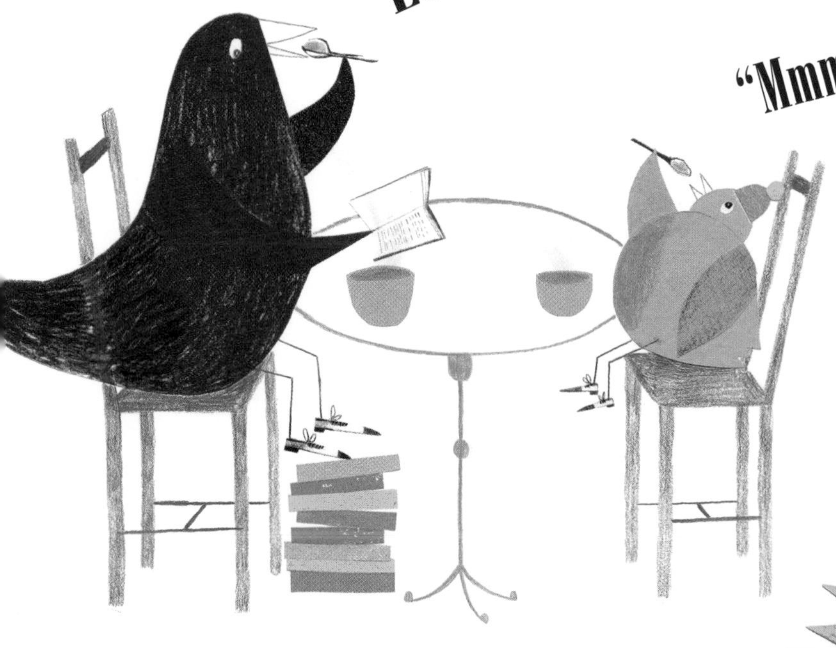

"Great soup, Harry.

Terrific!"

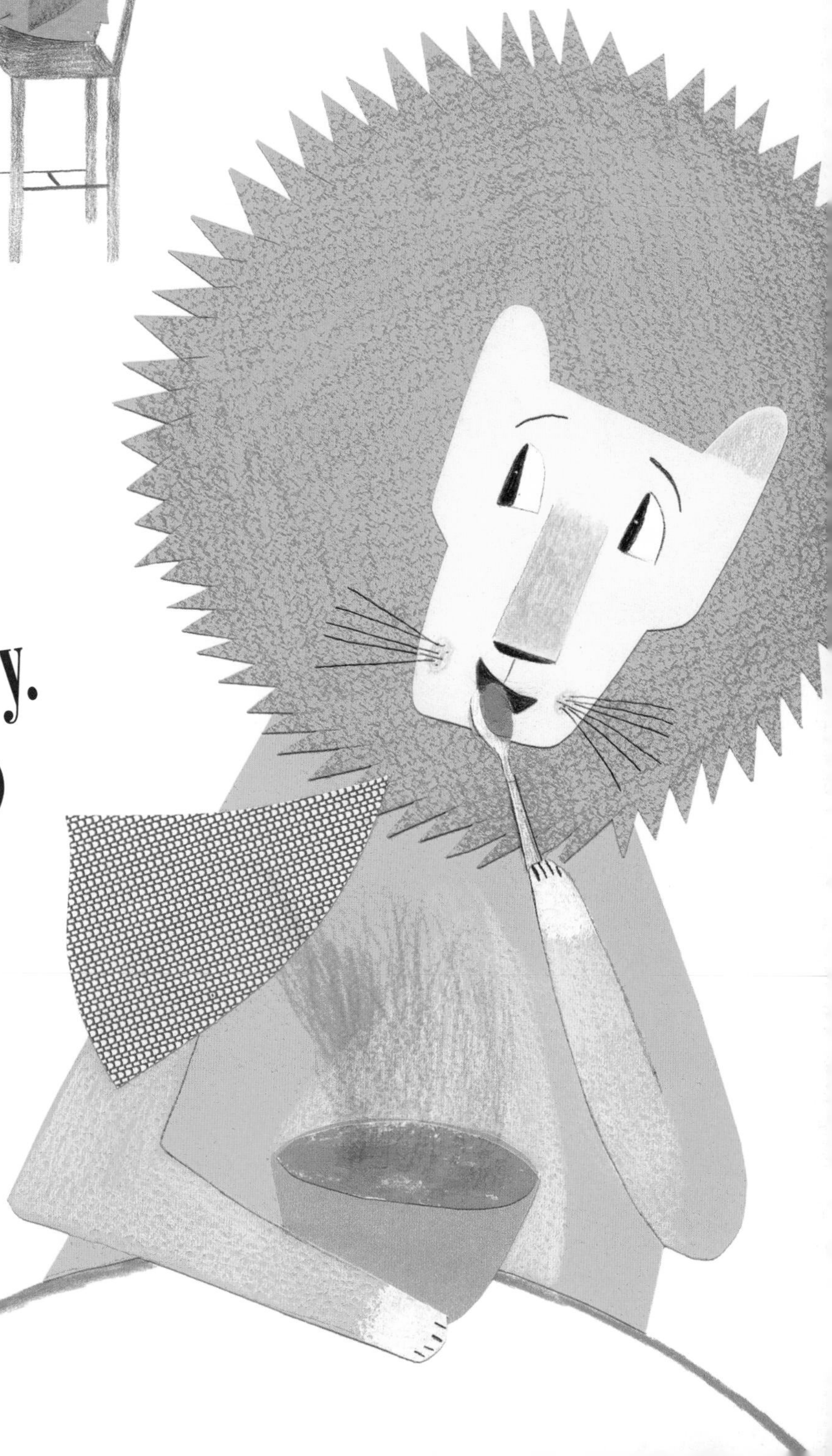

Harry is happy.
He's Happy Harry.

But what about Matt?
Something's wrong with Matt.

"Hey,
Harry,"
says Matt.
"The
soup's
no good."

WANTED
$1000

Daily Miaow

"WHAT?!"
says
Harry.
"Everyone
loves my
soup."

"You come and try it,
Harry,"
says Matt.

"OK, Matt,"

says

Harry.
"I'll try it."

"Hey, Matt," says Harry. "There's no spoon. You haven't got a spoon."

"That's it, Harry!"

says Matt.

"There's no spoon.

I haven't got a spoon.

That's what's wrong with the

soup,

Harry."

Daily Miaow

Everyone laughs about the
soup
with no spoon.

Ha Ha Ha!

Ha Ha Ha!

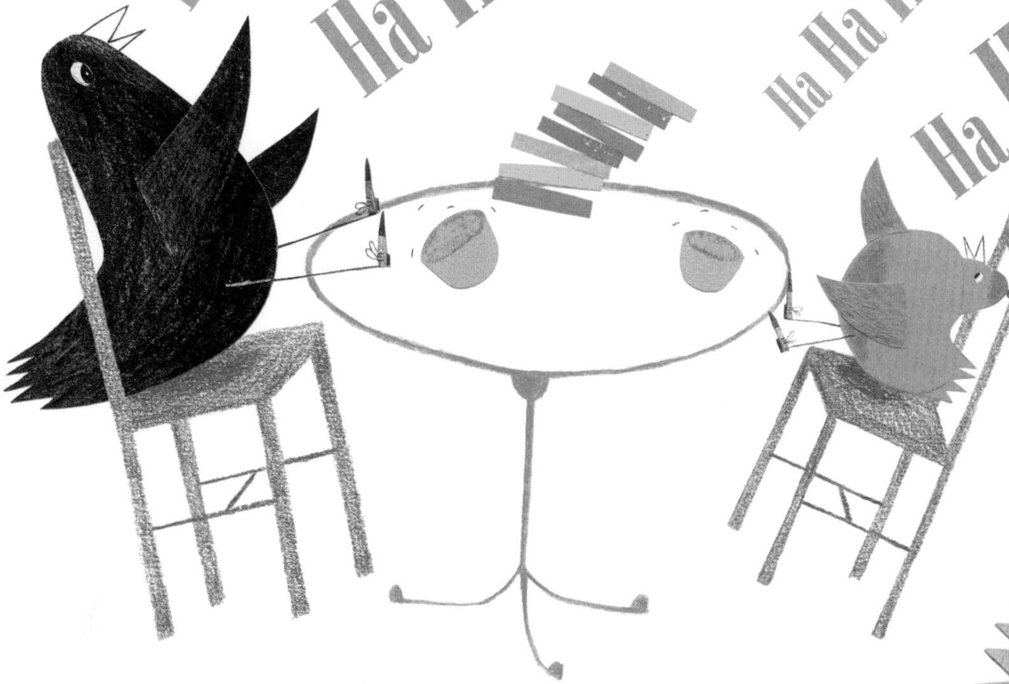

Ha Ha Ha!

Ha Ha Ha!

Ha Ha Ha!

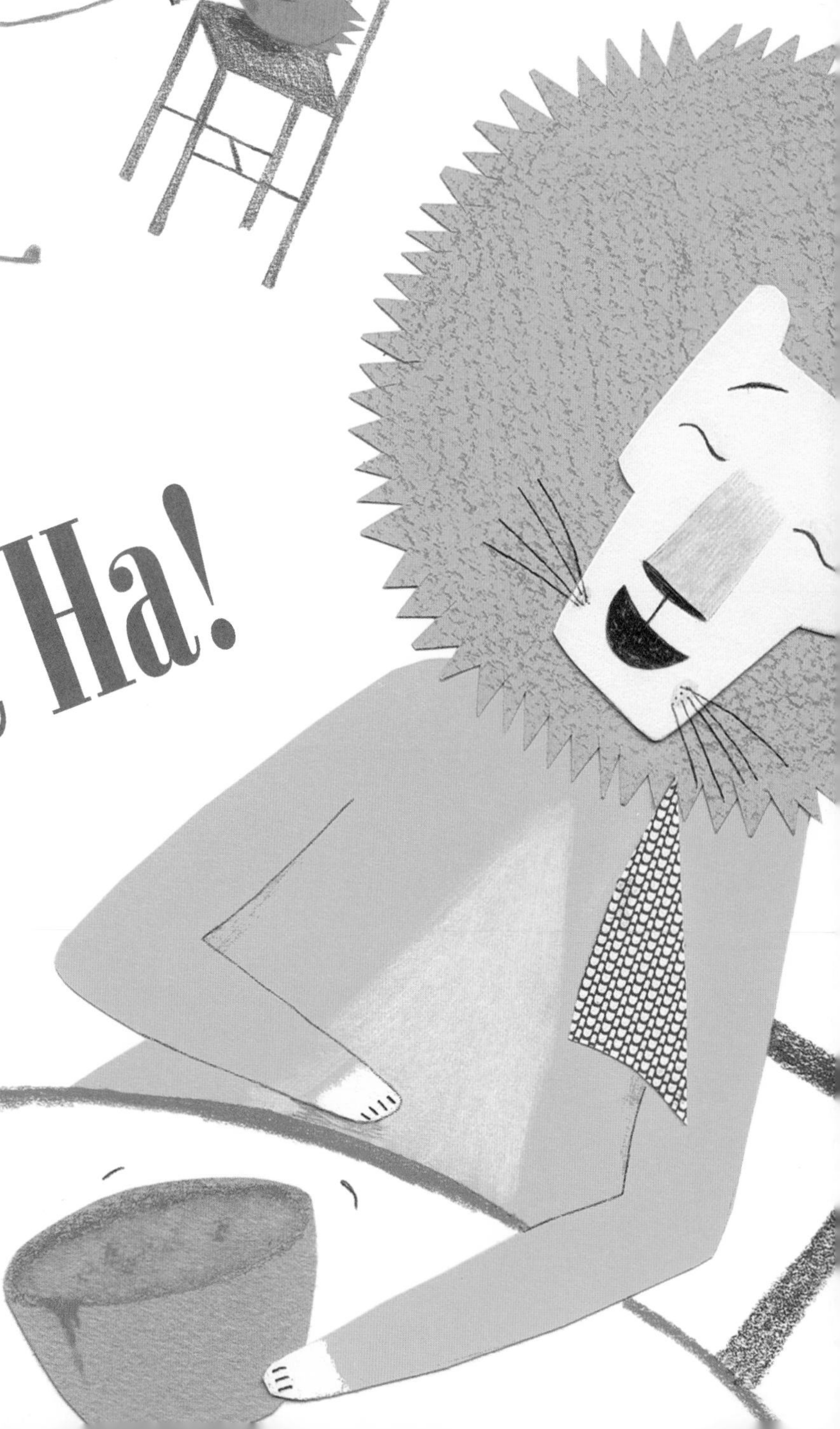

Harry gives Matt a spoon.

"You know something?" says Matt.

"What?" says Harry.

"Great

soup,

Harry!"

says Matt.

And...

Harry an

soup

If you don't have a spoor

If you can't taste the soup

So would I like a spoon?

Do you like the soup?

The soup is good

The soup is good

The soup is good

Matt sing a

song:

you can't taste the soup.

the soup's no good.

Oh yes I would.

Oh the soup is good.

The soup is good.

The soup is good.

The soup is good.

Everyone joined in
and everyone was happy at

Happy

HARRY'S

Café.